First published by Parragon in 2013

Parragon
Chartist House
15–17 Trim Street
Bath BA1 1HA, UK
www.parragon.com

Written by Frances Prior-Reeves
Designed by Talking Design
Illustrations by Eleanor Carter

ISBN 978-1-4723-1130-6
Printed in China

Oodles of Doodles

PaRragon

Bath • New York • Singapore • Hong Kong • Cologne • Delhi
Melbourne • Amsterdam • Johannesburg • Shenzhen

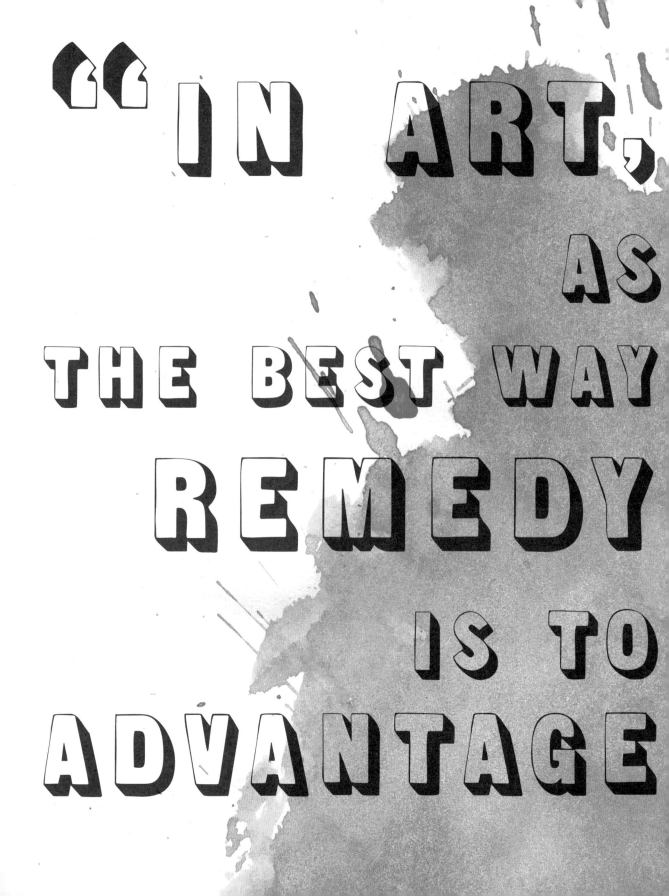

"IN ART, AS THE BEST WAY REMEDY IS TO ADVANTAGE

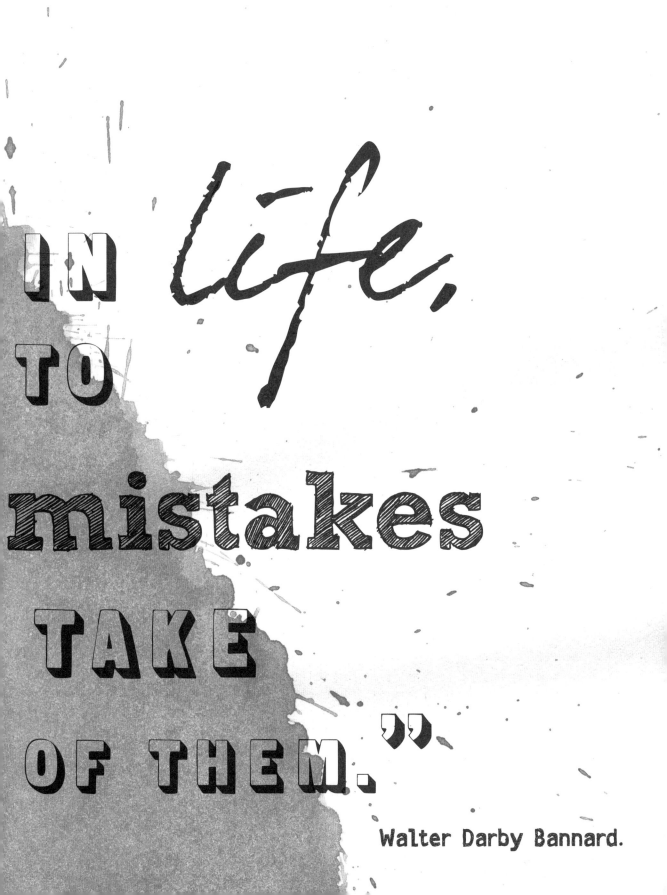

Fill this page with **spirals**, what happens when they overlap?

Can you create a **whirlpool** of color?

Draw this *bird's song.*

Color this **PATTERN,** making sure that any segments that touch aren't in the same **COLOR.**

Draw your **happiest** mood.

Draw your **SADDEST** mood.

Draw your angriest mood.

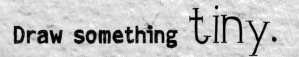

Draw something tiny.

Draw something

GIGANTIC.

Draw without
RESTRICTIONS.

Draw your
IDEA.

Draw a **target** using only SQUARES.

Draw a brick wall using only
CIRCLES.

What does the color **GREEN** look like in love?

What does the color
blue look like sunbathing?

DRAW!

Create a list of

WORDS

about a waterfall.

Flow those words into an IMAGE.

Draw your favorite song.

Draw your favorite **BAND.**

Draw an animal that combines your five favorite animals.

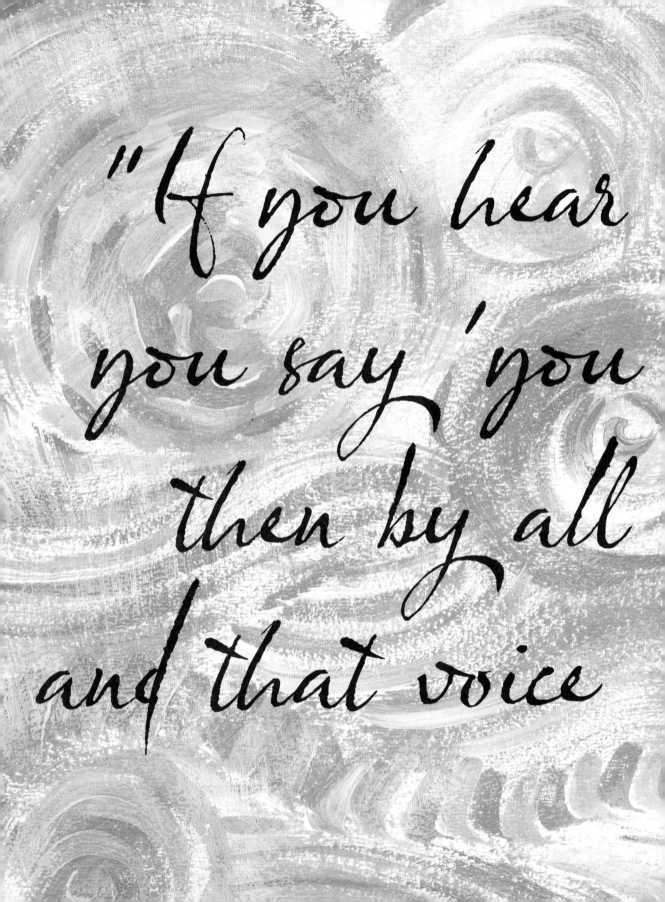

"If you hear
you say 'you
then by all
and that voice

a voice within
cannot paint,'
means paint,
vill be silenced."

Vincent Van Gogh.

Doodles
don't have to
be mindless.

Draw a portrait of yourself in **disguise.**

Draw the thing that goes **BUMP** in the night.

BE CREATIVE!

Draw a **Jealous** color.

Draw a **calm** color.

Draw  **PURPLE** and **yellow** in love.

Draw once upon a **time.**

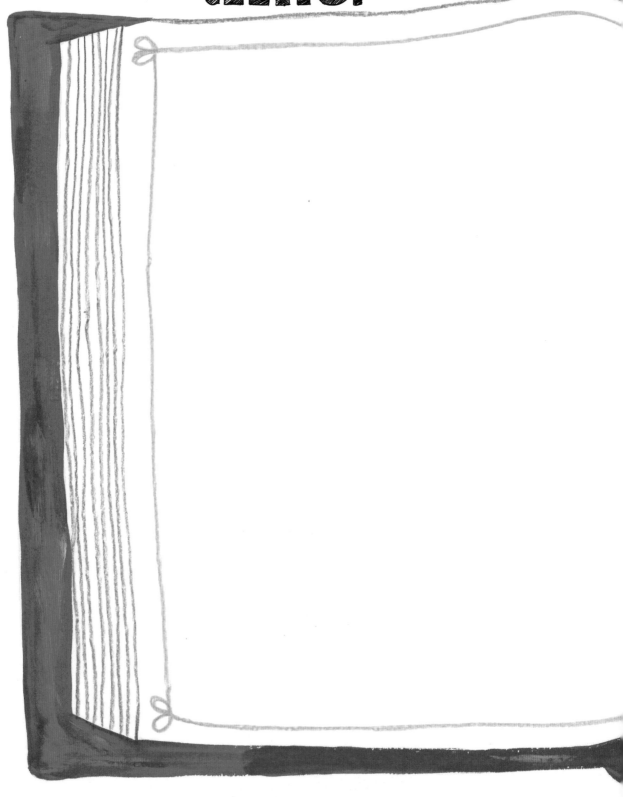

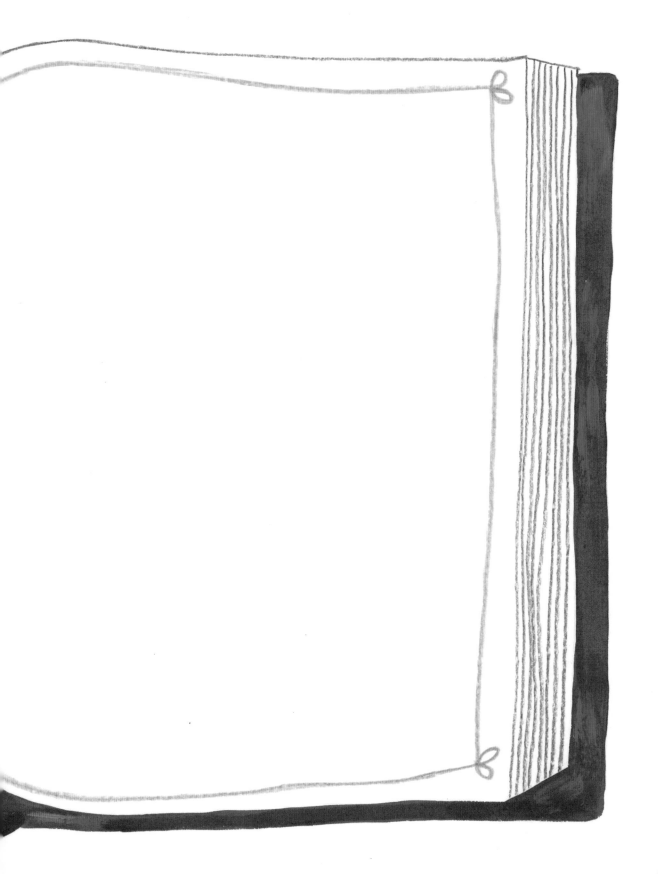

Fill these pages with shapes with
more than **FIVE SIDES.**

Draw a *mirage.*

"I found I could say things with color and shapes that I couldn't say any other way— things I had no words for."

Georgia O'Keeffe.

Draw your MOOD using one continuous line.

1 2 3 4 5 6 7 8 9 10 11 12 13 14 15 16 17 18 19 20 21 22 23 24 25 26 27 28 29 30

COLOR!

Fill this grassland with *life*.

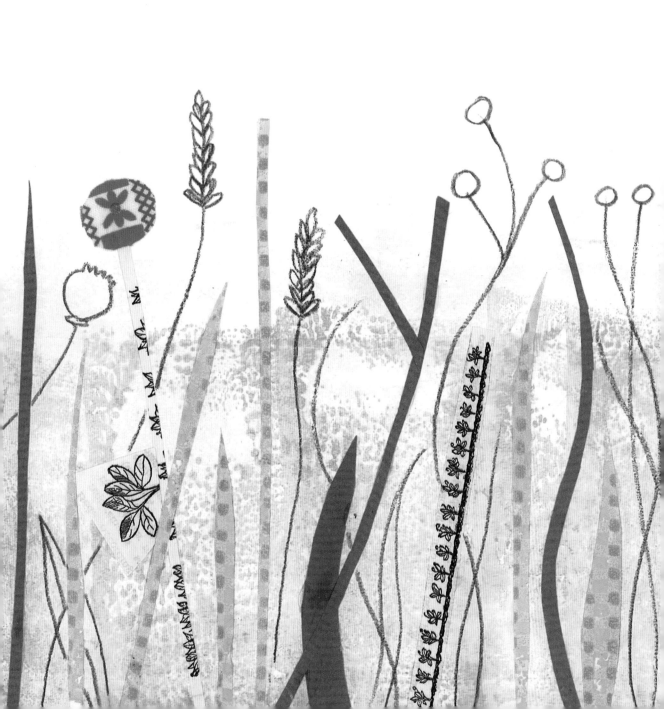

Draw the  you've just had.

Create a pattern using
different types of STARS.

Space for your
creativity.

Draw your favorite BOOK.

Draw your favorite SERIES.

Draw something HAIRY.

SHADE these pages and
then use an eraser to cut through it and
create something beneath.

Create a list of **words** about the **rainforest.**

Grow those words into an

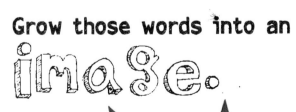

Draw a reflection in this
PUDDLE.

Fill this *night sky* with stars.

SCRIBBLE!

Draw a **striped spot.**

Draw a **SPOTTED STRIPE.**

Draw a striped dalmation.

Draw a spotted TIGER.

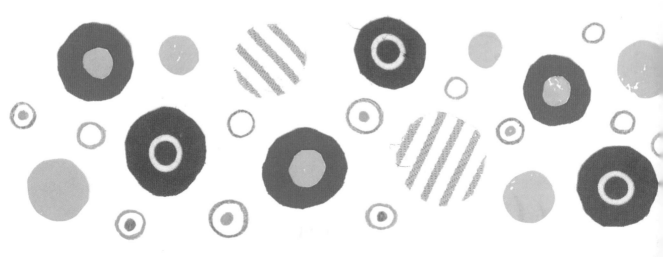

Personalize
this space.

Look around and pick out
everything
that is blue.

Draw *everything* you

see in that color in

ONE PICTURE.

Draw a *windy day.*

Draw something **WIDE.**

Draw something NARROW.

"Think left and
and think low
Oh, the thinks
up if only you

think right and think high. you can think try."

Dr. Seuss.

Draw a

DIAMOND
spinning.

Draw a *ZIGZAG* waving.

Draw a **triangle**
doing cartwheels.

Draw a **GEOMETRIC** TESSELLATING pattern.

Draw the *view*

from your

window.

Draw the view from

OUTSIDE

your window

looking in.

Create a new **font** that shows your *personal* style.

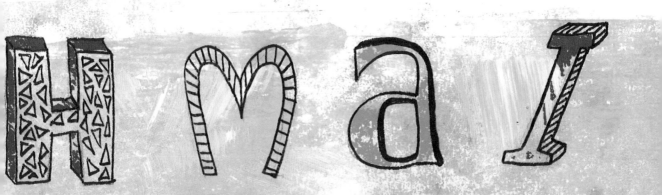

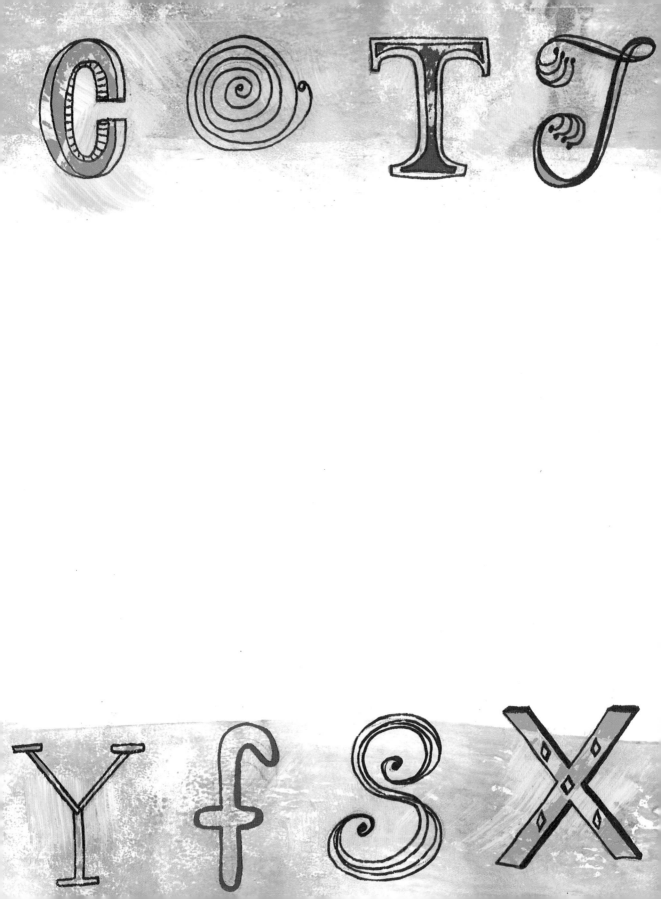

Drawing is creating!

Assign **MOODS** to each color.

If you **INVERT** these what would
happen to the mood of a picture?

"I've been 40 years discovering that the queen of all colors was black."

Pierre-Auguste Renoir.

Draw your *happiest* memory.

Draw something *shiny.*

Sketch!

Add a row of **exotic birds**
to this branch in BLACK AND WHITE.

Draw a **CHESSBOARD,** *piano,* and a newspaper using only primary colors.

Space for
your art.

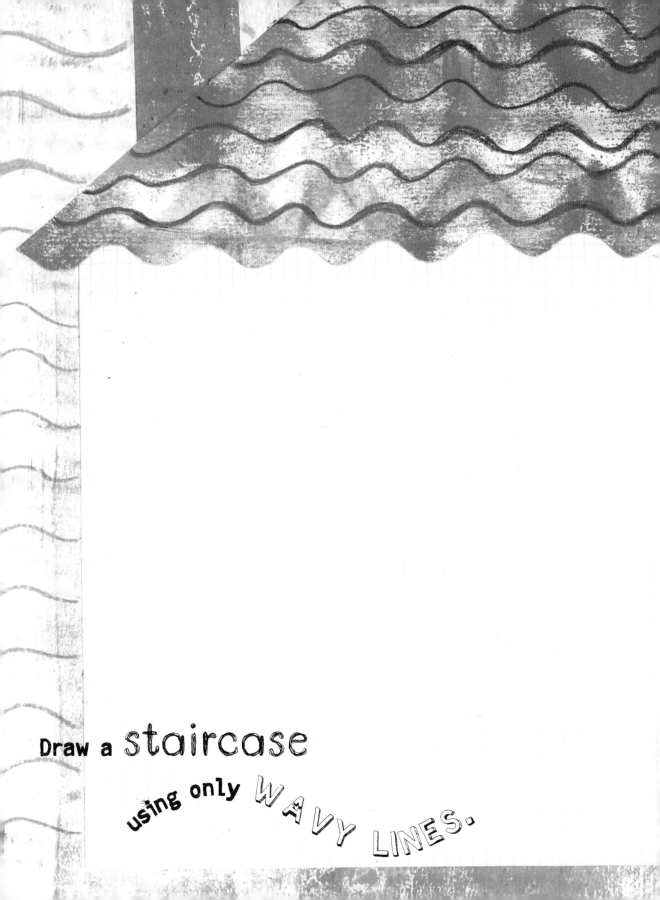

Draw a staircase using only WAVY LINES.

Draw the OCEAN

using only diagonal lines.

Draw what's **directly in front** of you using one continuous line.

Create a list of words about

CLOUDS.

Float

those words into an image.

Draw an **ANT** the size of a house.

Draw an oak tree the size of a grass seed.

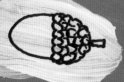
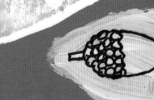

Draw a **bird in a tree** in
BLUE and *green* tones.

Draw a **bird in a tree** in
red and **ORANGE** tones.

what changes?

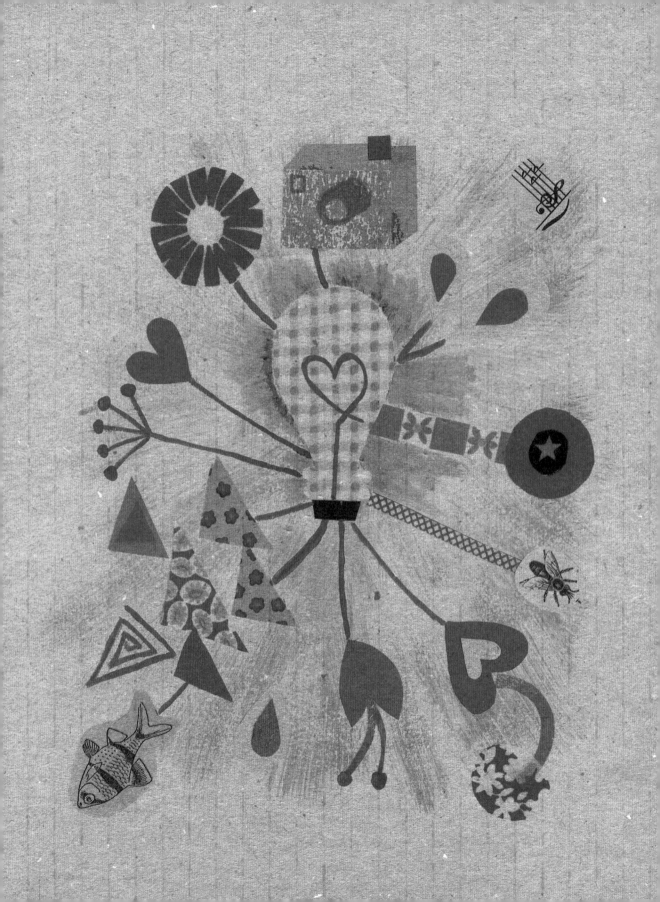

"Creativity is
INTELLIGENCE
having fun."

Albert Einstein.

Draw the ending to your **adventure story** here.

Fill this page with a nighttime
CITYSCAPE.

Draw your favorite
TV SHOW.

Draw your favorite MOVIE.

DON'T
THINK
JUST
DRAW.

Doodle!

Draw a *portrait* of yourself from the back.

Draw a portrait of yourself upside down.

Draw what is at the BOTTOM of this well.

Draw something **you're looking forward to.**

Light a
campfire.

Draw the **SMOKE** billowing onto this page.

Look around and pick
out everything that is

Draw everything you
see in that **color**
in one picture.

Draw something
beginning with
the letter **X**

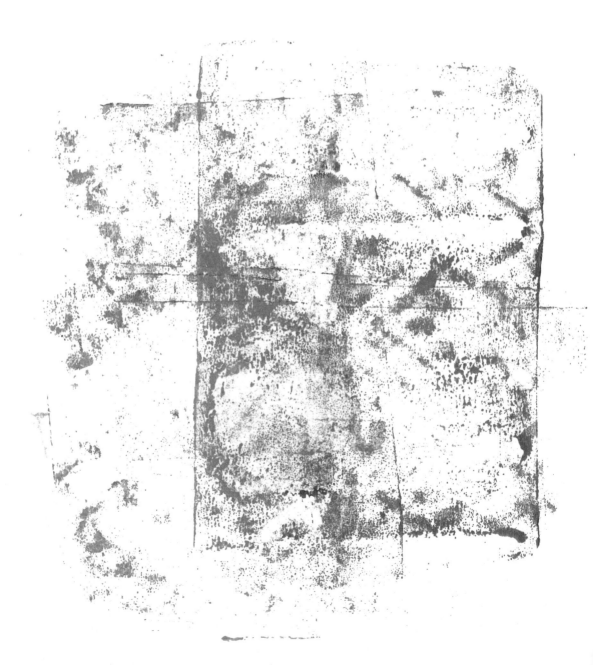

Draw something
beginning with
the letter

Draw an *ecstatic* color.

Draw a **SAD** color.

Draw PINK and
RED in a fight.

CREATE!

Fill THESE PAGES with as many ideas as you can ...

There are
no limits.

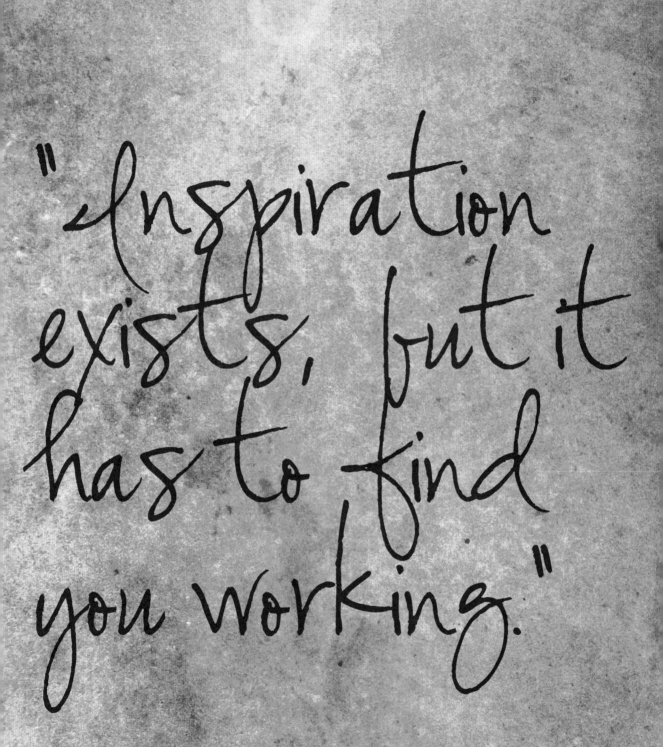

"Inspiration exists, but it has to find you working."

Pablo Picasso.